The Roly-Poly Rice Ball

By Penny Dolan

Illustrated by Diana Mayo

Special thanks to our advisers for their expertise:

Adria F. Klein, Ph.D.
Professor Emeritus, California State University
San Bernardino, California

Susan Kesselring, M.A.
Literacy Educator
Rosemount-Apple Valley-Eagan (Minnesota) School District

PICTURE WINDOW BOOKS
Minneapolis, Minnesota

Levels for *Read-it!* Readers

- Familiar topics
- Frequently used words
- Repeating patterns

- New ideas
- Larger vocabulary
- Variety of language structures

- Challenges in ideas
- Expanded vocabulary
- Wide variety of sentences

- More complex ideas
- Extended vocabulary range
- Expanded language structures

A Note to Parents and Caregivers:

Read-it! Readers are for children who are just starting on the amazing road to reading. These beautiful books support both the acquisition of reading skills and the love of books.

The RED LEVEL presents familiar topics using common words and repeating sentence patterns.

The BLUE LEVEL presents new ideas using a larger vocabulary and varied sentence structure.

The YELLOW LEVEL presents more challenging ideas, a broad vocabulary, and wide variety in sentence structure.

The GREEN LEVEL presents more complex ideas, an extended vocabulary range, and expanded language structures.

When sharing a book with your child, read in short stretches, pausing often to talk about the pictures. Have your child turn the pages and point to the pictures and familiar words. And be sure to reread favorite stories or parts of stories.

There is no right or wrong way to share books with children. Find time to read with your child, and pass on the legacy of literacy.

Adria F. Klein, Ph.D.
Professor Emeritus
California State University
San Bernardino, California

First American edition published in 2005 by
Picture Window Books
5115 Excelsior Boulevard
Suite 232
Minneapolis, MN 55416
877-845-8392
www.picturewindowbooks.com

First published in Great Britain by Franklin Watts, 96 Leonard Street,
London, EC2A 4XD

Printed in the United States of America.

Library of Congress Cataloging-in-Publication Data
Dolan, Penny.
The Roly-poly rice ball / written by Penny Dolan ; illustrated by Diana Mayo.
p. cm. — (Read-it! readers)
Summary: Li sits down under a cherry tree to eat his lunch of three rice balls,
but when they jump off of his lap and roll down a hole, Li rolls down after them
and finds a tiny surprise.
ISBN 1-4048-0914-7 (hardcover)
[1. Mice—Fiction.] I. Mayo, Diana, ill. II. Title. III. Series.
PZ8.D669Ro 2004
[E]—dc22
2004009182

All morning, Li swept the path
clean for the rich people to walk on.

Then Li sat under the cherry tree
and unfolded his lunch cloth.
There lay three rice balls, as white
and round as three tiny moons.

Li sighed. His rice box at home was now empty. What would he eat for supper tonight?

Suddenly, Li heard tiny voices singing: "Roly-poly rice ball, roly-poly rice ball, roly-poly rice ball, roll right IN!"

One rice ball jumped off Li's cloth
and rolled down a hole under the
cherry tree.

The voices sang
again: "Roly-poly
rice ball, roll right IN!" Li saw
his second rice ball roll
down the hole.
Then the third!

Li bent down and heard
laughing and singing
coming from the hole.

"I hope you enjoy my rice balls,
whoever you are!" he cried.

"Roly-poly rice ball,
roll right IN!"
came the voices.
And this time,
Li went rolling
down the hole!

Li rolled into a tiny underground
palace. Lots of mice, dressed in fine
robes, nibbled away at Li's rice balls.

16

The mouse emperor sat high on his
throne. He smiled at Li. Li smil
back, though he felt very hungr

The emperor clapped his paws.
The old mice played music on tiny
instruments. The music was as sweet
as the birds singing in the cherry tree.

The emperor smiled. So did Li,
though he was still very hungry.

Then the young mice danced
together, waving their painted
fans. They were as pretty as petals
fluttering from the cherry tree.

The emperor smiled at Li again.

Li smiled, too, though by now

he was very hungry indeed.

"Friend Li," said the emperor. "You gave us rice balls for our feast, and you welcomed our singing and dancing. One thing more?"

"Just ask!" said Li.

"Now that our feast is over, will you sweep everywhere clean again?" asked the emperor.

Li knew the mice were only little,
so he was happy to help them clean
the palace. He hoped that sweeping
would stop his hunger.

The mice brought a brush and
a sack. Then they scurried off,
squeaking with laughter.

When Li knelt to sweep away the crumbs, he saw piles of long lost jewels and coins lying there.

"Take that rubbish away, Friend
Li," said the emperor, smiling.
"Mice do not need such things!"

27

As Li swept the last coin into the sack, he heard that song again:

"Roly-poly rice ball, roly-poly
rice ball, roly-poly rice ball,
roll right OUT!"

And Li was back under the
cherry tree, with his own
good fortune beside him.
He was never
hungry again.

Levels for *Read-it!* Readers

Read-it! Readers help children practice early reading
skills with brightly illustrated stories.

Red Level: Familiar topics with frequently used words and
repeating patterns.
I Am in Charge of Me by Dana Meachen Rau
Let's Share by Dana Meachen Rau

Blue Level: New ideas with a larger vocabulary and a variety
of language structures.
At the Beach by Patricia M. Stockland
The Playground Snake by Brian Moses

Yellow Level: Challenging ideas with an expanded vocabulary
and a wide variety of sentences.
Flynn Flies High by Hilary Robinson
Marvin, the Blue Pig by Karen Wallace
Moo! by Penny Dolan
Pippin's Big Jump by Hilary Robinson
The Queen's Dragon by Anne Cassidy
Sounds Like Fun by Dana Meachen Rau
Tired of Waiting by Dana Meachen Rau
Whose Birthday Is It? by Sherryl Clark

Green Level: More complex ideas with an extended vocabulary
range and expanded language structures.
Clever Cat by Karen Wallace
Flora McQuack by Penny Dolan
Izzie's Idea by Jillian Powell
Naughty Nancy by Anne Cassidy
The Princess and the Frog by Margaret Nash
The Roly-Poly Rice Ball by Penny Dolan
Run! by Sue Ferraby
Sausages! by Anne Adeney
Stickers, Shells, and Snow Globes by Dana Meachen Rau
The Truth About Hansel and Gretel by Karina Law
Willie the Whale by Joy Oades

A complete list of *Read-it!* Readers is available on our Web site:
www.picturewindowbooks.com